This igloo book belongs to:

......................................

# Contents

Published in 2020
First published in the UK by Igloo Books Ltd
An imprint of Igloo Books Ltd
Cottage Farm, NN6 0BJ, UK
Owned by Bonnier Books
Sveavägen 56, Stockholm, Sweden
www.igloobooks.com

Illustrated by Lizzie Walkley
Written by Stephanie Moss
Cover designed by Victoria Watson
Interiors designed by Justine Ablett
Edited by Melanie Joyce

1020 002
2 4 6 8 10 9 7 5 3
ISBN 978-1-80022-491-9

Printed and manufactured in China

# Stories for 3 Year Olds

igloobooks

# Timmy's Toys

**TOOT-TOOT!** went Timmy,
with his toy train set.

**WHOOSH!** went his
brilliant, new toy jet.

**WHIZZ!** went Timmy,
with his race car, too.

But none of his playtimes
ever **really** came true.

So, he closed his eyes and **wished** to fly up high.
Next thing he knew, he was **looping-the-loop** through the sky!

Dipping and diving...

... and **swooping** down low.

There were lots of places Timmy could go.

Then, before Timmy knew it, he was somewhere new.
In his very own train, past hills and fields he flew.

TOOT-TOOT! went the train,
as Timmy pulled on the cord.
He called to the passengers,
**"Come on, all aboard!"**

Racing through tunnels, the train went CLICKETY-CLACK!
It **whizzed** and **zoomed** along the twisty train track.

PUFF-PUFF! went the steam, flying into the air.
Timmy called to the farmer and said,
**"Hello, there!"**

In the blink of an eye, Timmy was behind his car wheel.
**"This is the best fun ever!"** he cried, with a squeal.

ZIP! went the race car as he **zoomed** round a bend.
He didn't **ever** want this adventure to end.

**"Time for tea!"** called Mum,
as Timmy opened his eyes.
He was back in his bedroom,
much to his surprise.

He'd had a **wonderful** adventure with his car, jet and train.
Timmy knew that playtime would **never** be the same.

9

# Fairyland

**"Are fairies real?"** asked Amy one day.
She had come to Grandma's house to play.

Grandma said, **"Yes!"** and didn't Amy know?
She told her there are fairies everywhere you go!

They hide behind plant pots, in flowers, in trees.
They **flit** and **flutter** along on the breeze.

Fairy dust falls from their wands with a **flick.**

**"To see them,"** she said, **"you have to be quick."**

**"Oh, I DO!"** said Amy with a cry.
**"I want to be a fairy and I want to fly!"**

**"Well,"** said Grandma, **"then you must sing
and make a wish in the fairy ring."**

As Grandma went off to have a rest, Amy put her **wishing** to the test.

In the fairy ring, eyes closed **tight**,
she **sang** and **wished** with all her might.

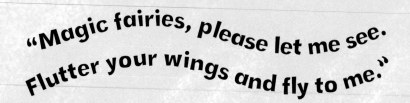

"Magic fairies, please let me see.
Flutter your wings and fly to me."

Suddenly, there was a **tinkling** sound.
Little fairies were flying around.

14

**"Hello, Amy,"** they said. **"How nice to meet you. We are Bluebell, Daisy and Sparkle, too."**

They **sprinkled** fairy dust and took Amy by the hand. **"Away!"** they cried. **"To Fairyland."**

15

Fairyland was like a **magical** dream,
where trees were candy and flowers, ice cream.

The fairies made magic. ZAP! ZING! PING!
**"Wow!"** cried Amy. **"I've got fairy wings!"**

She zoomed and darted here and there.
"Whoo-hoo!" cried Amy, as she whizzed through the air.

She found the prettiest tree house she had ever seen.
It was the magical palace of the fairy queen.

The fairy queen showed Amy all around.
Then they gently **fluttered** down to the ground.

**"Let's have a fairy feast,"** the fairy queen said.
**"Then after that, it will be time for bed."**

So, the fairies feasted on **magical** food.
Then they danced around the **enchanted** wood.

The fairy bells **tinkled** and it was time to sleep.

**"Sssh, little fairies,"** said the fairy queen.
**"Not a peep."**

Amy said goodnight to all her fairy friends.
She didn't want her magic **adventure** to end.

"**Goodnight,**" said Bluebell, Daisy and Sparkle, too.
"**We're so glad to be friends with you.**"

When Amy woke, she was in the fairy ring.
Of her fairies, she remembered **everything**.

"Thank you, fairies," she whispered and off she ran.
"What an amazing adventure.
I can't wait to tell Gran!"

# Rainbow Play Park

If you want to go out and have **fun** for the day,
Rainbow Play Park is the **perfect** place to play.

WELCOME

Grab Mummy and Daddy and your **best** teddy, too.
Then choose your first ride, there's **so** much to do!

You can **jump** on the roundabout, starting off slow.

Then **spin** round faster, as quick as you can go!

Up and down, up and down, on the **bouncy** see-saw.

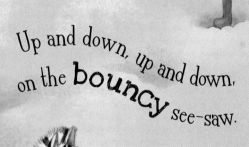

You'll feel like you've **never** had so much fun before.

You can **SCRAMBLE** up the climbing frame, right to the top.
Go on, nearly there, you can do it, don't stop!

Then you can sneak
into the playhouse...

...shhh, quick, hide!

Next, you
**whizz**
and
**zoom**
down the slippery slide.

Flying backwards and forwards, **high** up on the swing,
you'll feel like you can do almost anything.

**"Giddy up!"** you say, on the **bouncy** play horse.
Where to next? It's the sandpit, of course!

Jumping on the trampoline,
you **fly** into the air.
Bouncing and **soaring**
without a single care.

Then you swing across the monkey bars, one, two, three.
**"I made it!"** you cry. **"Mummy, look at me!"**

When it's time to go, at the end of the day,
**"I was having so much fun!"** you say.

GOODBYE

With so many **exciting** things to do and see,
Rainbow Play Park **really** is the place to be.

# Candyland

**"Yuck!"** said little Billy,
when he saw his tea one night.

His twin sister, Bella,
wouldn't even take one bite.

She shook her head and said, **"I wish we had sweets for tea!"**
**"Your wish might come true,"** said Billy. **"Follow me."**

28

They went to the pantry and opened the door.
When they looked inside, their mouths fell to the floor.

Instead of shelves of food, much to their surprise,
they saw a SECRET land of candy, right before their eyes.

There were rivers made of chocolate
with waterfalls of cream.

There were lollies, sweets and jellies.
It was better than a dream!

**"Wheee!"**
cried Billy,
**whooshing**
down the waterfall.

**"Wait for me!"** called Bella.
She could hardly wait at all.

There was a palace
made of cookies...

... and a valley
made of sweets.

Ice creams towered over them,
as they walked down Candy Street.

The clouds were made
of candyfloss...

... the sun a
blueberry pie.

So they
bounced
and tumbled into the valley.

Next, they raced through Lolly Meadow and slid down Hot Fudge Hill.
They ate everything in sight, until they'd had their fill.

**"I feel a bit too full,"**
said Bella, clutching at her belly.

**"I think we'd better go,"**
said Billy, putting down his jelly.

As soon as they made a wish, they both shut their eyes tight, and found themselves back home, where everything felt just right.

**"That was the best adventure ever!"** said Billy, with a smile.

**"Yes,"** said Bella, **"but I don't want sweets for quite a while."**

33

# Magic Mummy

My mummy can't fly and she doesn't have wings,
but I think she can do **magical** things.

No one else around can see,
but everything she does is **amazing** to me.

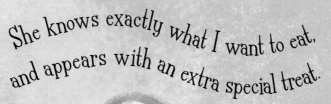

She knows exactly what I want to eat,
and appears with an extra special treat.

She makes cakes that
come out of thin air.

whisk,
whizz,
whirr
and they are there.

She knows just what to get me for my birthday.

"Mummy, how did you know?" I say.

"That's what mummies are for," she replies, with a magic twinkle in her eyes.

She seems to know exactly
what I think.
Before I've said I'm thirsty,
she'll bring me a drink.

If I'm outside playing
hide-and-seek,
she finds me without
even taking one peek.

Mummy can tell when I'm feeling sad.
She gives me a hug, so I don't feel so bad.

Sometimes I think she can read my mind.
If I'm lonely, she's **never** far behind.

At the top of the slide, she holds me **tight**.
Suddenly I know it will be alright.

Then I whizz down. woohoo, weee!

She makes me feel as
**brave** as can be.

My mummy is **special** in the best way,
when I'm happy, or sad and when we play.

She's always right there for me,
exactly when I need her to be.

No one has a mummy like I do. She makes all my **wishes** come true.
Because she knows just how I feel, I know that her **magic** really is real.

# Up All Night

If I didn't have to go to sleep,
when Daddy says,

**"Shhh now, not a peep."**

There are so many fun things I would do
instead of sleeping the whole night through.

I'd **tiptoe** along the bedroom floor...

... go to the wardrobe and open the door.

Inside, hiding behind my clothes...

... would be lots of feet with

# hairy toes.

They'd belong to **monsters** of every kind.
They'd **smell** a bit, but I wouldn't mind.

We'd do somersaults on my bed.

"**Watch out!**" I'd cry.
"**Mind your head!**"

44

Then I'd take out **every** toy in my chest.
The soldiers are the ones I like best.

We'd parade in our **marching** band,
with the other toys at my command.

45

I'd **draw** and **scribble** like never before,
and cover my walls with pictures galore.

I'd watch them as they'd **glimmer** and **glow**.
They'd come to life and put on a show!

I'd **draw** and **scribble** like never before,
and cover my walls with pictures galore.

I'd watch them as they'd **glimmer** and **glow**.
They'd come to life and put on a show!

Then I'd take out **every** toy in my chest.
The soldiers are the ones I like best.

We'd parade in our **marching** band,
with the other toys at my command.

45

Along would come a **magical** friend.
Our night-time fun would never end.

We'd **fly** round the garden,
to the stars and back.

We'd **even** stop at the moon,
for a snack.

I'd stay up having **fun** until dawn.
Then, suddenly, I'd begin to yawn.

**"Time for bed,"**

my monster friend would call.

**"Little lions need
their sleep after all."**